GW01159026

Cotton
Cleopatra
F VIII

The Abbess's Tale

Cotton
Cleopatra
F VIII

The Abbess's Tale

Dominic Selwood

CORAX

Published in Great Britain by
CORAX
London

Visit our author website
www.dominicselwood.com

Copyright © Dominic Selwood 2022

The right of Dominic Selwood to be identified as author of this work has been asserted in accordance with Section 77 of the Copyright, Designs and Patents Act 1988.

All rights reserved. This book is copyright material and no part of this publication may be reproduced, downloaded, decompiled, reverse engineered, photocopied, recorded or stored in or transferred into any information storage and/or retrieval system, or transmitted, in any form or by any means, whether electronic or mechanical, now known or hereafter invented, without the prior express written permission of Corax, nor be otherwise circulated in any form of binding or cover other than that in which it is published and without a similar condition being imposed on the subsequent purchaser.

British Library Cataloguing in Publication Data.
A catalogue record for this book is available from the British Library.

ISBN 978-1-7390976-0-8 (print)

Typeset by Corax in Adobe Garamond Pro

About the Author

Dominic Selwood is a historian, journalist, and barrister. He is a bestselling author and novelist, and a frequent contributor to national newspapers, radio, and television. He has a doctorate in medieval history from the University of Oxford and a masters from the Sorbonne. He is a Fellow of the Royal Historical Society and the Society of Antiquaries. He lives in London.

He tweets at:
@DominicSelwood

A letter addressed to the London publishers Watkins & Brown of Cecil Court W.C.2, found among the copious papers of Iana Jenkins, F.B.A., D.PHIL., died Axminster, Wiltshire. 28 November 1970.

Sirs,

In the roaring 1920s — after the horrors and tragedies of the Great War, and the pestilential influenza from which, it seemed, no family could escape — we set about forging a new world. The University of Oxford played its part in this renaissance by admitting women to read for the degree of Doctor of Philosophy. I was fortunate to be in the first cohort, and set about researching the survival of Anglo-Saxon Church practices in the bloody aftermath of the Norman conquest. My good fortune was then extended by a fellowship at Somerville College, where I taught, most happily, my entire career. I do not care for the epithet "trailblazer" — there were very many like me —

but it is true I have always followed the less-trodden path.

Over the years, I have edited a wide range of volumes and monographs, with perhaps the most useful to scholars being the standard, critical editions of two invaluable texts by medieval English women writers: Julian of Norwich's *Revelations of Divine Love* and Margery Kempe's *Book of Margery Kempe*.

To my shame, however, there is one text by a medieval English woman I have never brought forward for publication. This has been principally for fear of recriminations, as the serene, green quadrangles of academia can be unforgiving places of rivalry and hostility, especially towards women of my generation.

Now I am retired, however, and able largely to spend my days cataloguing the copious collection of papers I have accumulated, I no longer mind that some may disbelieve, or even ridicule, me for the circumstances in which I came into possession of the work. I now feel that the importance of drawing this unique text to the public's attention outweighs what any sharp tongue may wish to say of me. Moreover, in truth, the work has never ceased to weigh down my waking and sleeping thoughts, and I can no longer carry its burden alone.

To understand all and form a judgement, you should know of the circumstances in which I found the text. Or perhaps — you may conclude after hearing the story — I should rightly say: in which the text found me.

During the war, like many others, I discontinued my teaching and settled in London to do my bit for the war effort. I volunteered with the Auxiliary Territorial Service, driving ambulances to convey those wounded in the bombings to hospital. At times the work was arduous and intense but, at others, there were lulls and, in these precious periods of respite, I walked from my lodgings in Marylebone to the British Museum, where I passed my days in the unrivalled ambience of the great, round reading room. My aim was to better acquaint myself with the Museum's extensive holding of medieval manuscripts, and the first task I set to was working through the great collection of Sir Robert Cotton M.P., which the Museum still, rather delightfully I have always thought, catalogues using the names of the Roman emperors and empresses whose marble busts once stood atop Cotton's book presses.

Arriving at the reading room one morning while working through Cotton's Empress Cleopatra class mark, I noted that the previous afternoon I had finished with *Cotton Cleopatra F VII*, which had proved to be a compendium of fifteenth- to early seventeenth-century noble titles from England, Italy, and Spain. Spanning such late dates, it was of little interest to me, but I had nonetheless persevered in case it held one of those rare gems of local or prosopographical information that can lead to an important connection or revelation. Now it was finished, I handed it back in at the high, wooden Enquiries Desk, and put in a chit for *Cotton Cleopatra F VIII*, then returned to my desk. I did not have too long to wait before I heard the wheels of the delivery trolley squeak up to my desk, and the benevolent assistant carefully placed the volume onto the faded, green, velvet book supports in front of me.

The book seemed unexceptional. Its red Morocco-wrapped boards were visibly eighteenth-century, and bore the clear, simple designation "Cotton Cleopatra F VIII" tooled in neat, small, gold lettering onto the spine. Original medieval bindings grow fragile, and libraries with the resources regularly replace those that have perished with more modern protective covers, as in this case. I therefore did not waste any time examining the volume's relatively modern binding.

Instead, with the sense of excited anticipation that every medievalist feels on opening an unfamiliar manuscript, I turned to the first page. It was not medieval vellum, but eighteenth-century paper which, to my joy, revealed itself to be a summary of contents inserted by whoever had undertaken the rebinding. These summary lists are always welcome, as they can otherwise take much effort to identify each text in such collections of assorted contents.

The list disclosed an array of ecclesiastical texts produced in the west of England from *circa* 1150 to 1250, which proved to be made up of the usual unconnected but colourful jumble that the ages throw into such volumes, assembled by some diligent medieval scholar or later bibliophile. Running my eye down it, I noted some scraps of liturgy, several calendars of regional feasts and fasts, a selection of hagiographies lauding local saints, a few grants of ecclesiastical privileges, the occasional *inspeximus*, and so on. However, around two-thirds into the list, one entry caused me to sit bolt upright in my chair.

The line read simply, "Mary Abbess of Shaftesbury's *Chronica wessexiensis*". I felt my face grow hot as I stared at the six words, taking them in slowly several times in case I had made an error. But I had not.

My heart began to race, because I knew for a fact that only one copy of Mary's *Chronica* had survived the ravages of the ages and the ideological book burnings of the Reformation. That sole surviving copy of the chronicle was now safely shelved in Lambeth Palace Library on the other side of the river Thames from where I was sitting. I knew of the Lambeth text because I had consulted it when reviewing the printed scholarly Latin-English edition that had been produced some fifteen years earlier by a friend and colleague, now dead. It was a singular text, as the great medieval chroniclers of England — Orderic Vitalis, Henry of Huntingdon, John of Salisbury, Roger of Howden, Matthew Paris, and the others — were all men, so the subtly different perspective and priorities of a female chronicler have always made Mary's work an important window into the age, a uniqueness enhanced by her unusually high status.

It seemed to me most likely that whoever had compiled the list of contents I was looking at had made an error, and simply mislabelled the text as Mary's *Chronica*. These things happened more often than one might think. But, at the back of my mind, I could not suppress an excitable inner voice hoping that I might have discovered a second version of Mary's chronicle entirely unknown to scholars.

It is every historian's waking and sleeping dream to stumble across an unknown copy of an important work. My mind was therefore already playing out what a splash it would be. So little is known of medieval women's writing in England that another manuscript would yield immensely important information. Did it pre- or post-date the Lambeth text? Was it copied by the same scribe or a different one? Did it originate in the same part of the country or elsewhere, or even abroad? Was it the exact same text, or were there small variations which might give clues as to the transmission and evolution of the chronicle? The answers to all these and other questions could make it the discovery of a lifetime for a medieval scholar.

With my heart in my mouth, I rapidly navigated my way through the volume, turning the stiff, crinkled vellum until I found the folio where the list of contents said the *Chronica* began. The section started with a short biography of Mary written out in a delightful and luxurious eighteenth-century copperplate. It noted that Mary of Shaftesbury was daughter to Geoffrey Plantagenet and half-sister to King Henry II of England. Nothing was known of her childhood but, once adult, she was active at court and in the country, with a keen mind that saw her correspond with leading religious figures of the age, including the nature-loving friar Francis of Assisi, who founded the Order of Poor Clares as well as the Franciscans, and the mystic Hildegard, abbess of St Rupert's at Bingen in the Rhineland.

The main event in Mary's life, the author noted, occurred in 1181, when she was appointed abbess of Shaftesbury Abbey in Dorset, then England's second wealthiest house of nuns. From this position of authority, she steered her community through the turmoil of the reigns of her nephews Kings Richard the Lionheart and John Lackland, weathering the violence of the First Barons' War, the chaos surrounding the Charter of Runnymede, and then the uncertainty after the seditious barons' gift of the throne to Prince Louis of France. As a writer, the biography stated, Mary was known for the *Chronica*, and also deemed by some a strong contender to be the contemporary poet "Mary of France". She died in 1216, the year King John went to his grave and his underage son, Henry III, took the embattled throne.

The biographical introduction before me said no more, and I turned over to the *Chronica* itself. As I did, the following folio came loose from the old stitching and into my hand. This was not un-common with old bindings, and I did not think anything of it, but carefully tucked the leaf back into the spine, noting it was a title page reading simply, "*Chronica marie abbatissa shaftesbiriensis*". I then turned over to what I hoped would be the first folio of the chronicle itself, and received my second profound shock of the morning.

The title page that had come loose a moment earlier was in a small, neat hand. The shape of its letters placed it undoubtedly in the late twelfth or early thirteenth century, yet it was not the usual, confident writing of a trained monastic scribe skilled at strong, regular, artful letters in the latest book hand fashion. Rather, it was in the tidy, neat, unostentatious hand of someone studious writing in their personal papers. I had therefore assumed it was the handwriting of some medieval librarian or compiler who added this page to Mary's chronicle as a frontispiece.

My astonishment came on seeing the opening page of the chronicle itself, and realizing that it, too, was in this same unassuming, private hand. I quickly skimmed ahead and confirmed, to my amazement, that the entire text was in this handwriting. By now I was a little dizzy at the extraordinary possibility that I might be holding the very sheets of vellum Mary had filled with her own handwriting as she composed the chronicle.

I began to read hungrily, at times feeling unsteady, and I found the text was as I remembered it from the Lambeth copy. Mary had an engaging style as a storyteller, with vivid and keenly observed descriptions captured in a Latin prose that was direct and flowing with no stuffiness or pretention. However, on reaching the place where the Lambeth text ended, I was dumbfounded to see that the text before me continued further. I counted up the pages, and estimated that it ran on for around another third again in length.

My mind, already racing away from me, now went into a spin from which I was struggling to think clearly. Was this extra section just something the writer had copied from elsewhere? Texts of the period often did not have titles or indications that a new work was beginning, so it may just have been the start of a different text. That was most likely, I told myself. But I could not suppress the hope that it might be a lost part of Mary's chronicle, or even another unknown work by her. I was, I recall, rather overwhelmed by now, and my eyes wandered up to the great dome of historic books all around me — that calm cocoon smelling of old leather and wood polish — and I could not help but feel that I might be on the precipice of a momentous discovery that would be added to the many seismic ones made in this great room of the nation's knowledge.

When my eyes scanned the first few lines of the new text, my excitement became almost uncontrollable on realizing that it was indeed a continuation of Mary's *Chronica* that did not appear in the Lambeth Palace Library manuscript. Before me, I was now certain, lay a text completely unknown to scholars.

I read on more eagerly than I believe I have ever read any text before but, after a few moments, I suddenly grew profoundly anxious, with images rushing through my mind of a bomb falling onto the library, or some other catastrophe. In those days there were no easily accessible photographic services in the Museum, and every English medieval historian is mindful of the calamitous fire in 1731 that destroyed so much of Cotton's collection of the nation's treasured manuscripts when housed in Westminster under the careless guardianship of Parliament. So I pulled a sheaf of blank foolscap from my bag, took out a fresh pencil, and began copying out the unknown portion of text, forcibly slowing myself to work accurately and restrain from rushing ahead.

This, then, translated into English, is the final section of Mary's chronicle. I have taken the liberty of turning its long passages of reported speech into direct speech to make them easier to read. I have also, in places, used modern idioms to give it life for an audience not accustomed to the rhythms of medieval writing. Other than that, what I am sending you is, I believe, the first English translation of the unknown and ghastly ending of Mary of Shaftesbury's *Chronica wessexiensis*.

Editor's note:

1. *Throughout Mary's manuscript there are references to the eight daily monastic services of prayer or "offices". The precise times of these varied by monastic order, country, century, and length of daylight hours. For the purpose of Mary's* Chronica, *the following can be assumed*: *Vigils at 3.00 A.M., Lauds followed by Prime at 6.00 A.M., Terce at 9.00 A.M., Sext at noon, None at 3.00 P.M., Vespers at 5.30 P.M., and Compline at around 8.00 P.M.*

2. *As was common with medieval chronicles, Mary weaves biblical quotations into her writing. In Dr Jenkins's letter these passages appear underlined. In keeping with typesetting conventions, they have been italicized in the following text.*

——————— oOo ———————

I N THE NAME of the holy and indivisible Trinity.
Amen.

The Evangelist reminds us that *he who walks in darkness knows not where he goes*, therefore we should all *walk while the light is here, lest darkness overtake us*.

In the year of the holy Incarnation eleven hundred and ninety-one, in the second year of the reign of our lord King Richard, and the first of our lord pope Celestine, monstrous and unspeakable things took place in the blessed Abbey of Saint Peter and Saint Paul at Glastonbury.

An account of these events has already been given by Gerald of Barry — that same cleric some call Gerald of Wales — who was, at the time, chaplain to the lord king. Yet his record of that hideous affair, like the false gospels of the Egyptians, is full of untruths, and makes no mention of the ghastly happenings I saw with my own eyes. I shall *therefore put away lying* and cleave to the commandment. *Let each one speak truth with his neighbour, as we are members of one another.*

It is true that the hideousness of what transpired defies comprehension. But that does not mean it should not be related for, as the Apostle explains, *Now we see only as a puzzle in a mirror*, and so it is not ignorance to acknowledge that there are mysteries beyond our understanding.

This, then, is an account of the unutterable things that took place in that ancient, holy abbey, near to where Saint Joseph of Arimathea planted the Holy Thorn after Our Lord's triumph over the grave, bringing the light of the Resurrection to these mist-swathed islands. I pray God to keep me true to what I saw and heard *for lying lips are an abomination to the Lord.*

Long before these events came to pass, an elderly bard of the Brittonic tongue vouchsafed a great secret to the lord King Henry FitzEmpress, my brother. He confided that the poets of old, who sang of the great Arthur and his feats of arms, revealed that the fabled king's final resting place in Avalon was at the site that is now Glastonbury Abbey, and that the storied warrior found eternal peace there between two stone pyramids sunken into the earth of those soft, western hills.

The lord king immediately informed the lord abbot of Glastonbury of this celebrated burial, but that indolent abbot was not a man given to action nor interest in the deeds of former times. Yet when my nephew the lord King Richard appointed a new abbot — our beloved in Christ, Henry of Sully — all changed, for Abbot Henry was filled with the zeal and energy of the Spirit, and vowed to honour the mortal remains of so great a hero as Arthur.

Abbot Henry therefore made earnest preparations, and appointed the holiest time of year for this endeavour, selecting the morning that fell two days following the sacred triduum of Easter. In solemn anticipation of the momentous discovery, the good abbot invited Gerald of Barry to be a witness on behalf of the lord king, and invited me, as a personal friend in religion he knew to be much engaged with the past deeds of this corner of the realm.

After all these years, I shudder still to recall the horrors of that Passiontide. But I know that I must leave a faithful account of them for those that follow, and may it not be as the Evangelist says, that *because I speak the truth, you do not believe me*. Instead let it be as the Apostle says, *that speaking the truth is love*.

I passed the solemnity of Holy Week at our beloved home in Shaftesbury witnessing the sacred Pascal mysteries with my good sisters in the Lord. Then, once the Light had returned for another year and the Sunday liturgies were concluded, the following day I made straight for ancient Glastonbury.

Together with my travelling companions, I passed through the western regions of the great willow forest, then on to the levels. It was a journey I always enjoyed, bringing to mind how, long ago, the great King Ælfred hid out in those woods, before mustering an army of loyal men of the west and defeating the heathen Danes, thereby preserving the light of the one, true faith for these islands.

Our company then journeyed into the land of apples, where the old name in those parts for the ubiquitous fruit, *aval*, had caused the region to be named Avalon. I remained lost in my reveries until eventually I spied the unmistakable rise of Glastonbury's great, ancient tor, crowned with the noble church of St Michael. It was said by the ancient Britons that deep in the earth beneath its mass lay the entrance to the otherworld they called

Annwn, which was guarded by fierce Gwynn ap Nudd with his mighty cauldron of rebirth. As my eyes settled on it, the tor seemed almost to reach heaven, so it therefore did not astonish me that, to the ancient mind, it also reached down into the other immortal realm, connecting the two. I gazed on in silent contemplation until eventually we arrived at the abbey's tall gates, where I was met by the brother cellarer, given our Order's kiss of peace, and settled into the guesthouse by nightfall.

After such a journey filled with the wonders of nature and the past, it pained me to behold again the pitiful husk of that once great abbey. I had known Glastonbury in the years of its manifest glory, when there was no collection of sacred buildings in England to rival its splendour. But now its preeminence lived on only in the minds of those who could recall its radiance for, seven years earlier, a great fire had ravaged each of its building, and what remained of the exalted abbey was horribly mutilated by the flames. The cloisters were blackened, with parts crumbled away, and many were its structures whose roofs were now mere boards and scaffolding. But by far the

most heart-rending loss was the once unparalleled church, that jewel of the abbey. Its glittering
magnificence had been gutted by the flames, and
much of it now lay unused, fallen into rubble and
left to nature like a fallow field. The choir and
high altar had been temporarily reconstructed after a fashion, but the temple's great walls were jag-
ged and charred, and all but a few of its once daz-
zling windows were patched over with planking.

The indomitable monks of that great abbey
were by now all accustomed to living among the
rebuilding works, and ever joyful in their daily
efforts to reconstruct the sacred precincts on an
even grander scale. And they had already made
great strides, for truly *I saw the holy city, a new
Jerusalem, coming down from Heaven from God
prepared as a bride adorned for her husband.* A new
chapel to Our Lady had already risen like a phoe-
nix from the flames, and truly it was a miracle of
serenity and majesty. The monks had adorned it
with the most daring vaulting, in the new pointed style, and it seemed almost alive with intricate
and vibrant patterns of traceried stone. Among
its soaring arches I saw here a carved flower, there
a human head, and all burnished in a rainbow

of painted hues. The new glass, too, was uncommonly exquisite, which seemed appropriate, as the area and its abbey had long ago taken its name from "glass", owing to the bright reflectiveness of the river that flowed around its surrounding marches. The new chapel was a marvel, and the imagination and dexterity of the craftsmen was a miracle. All who saw it wondered that such things were possible by the labour of human hands. Truly the chapel shone as a beacon of salvation, testifying to the ineffable wonder of Heaven and the indestructibility and permanence of the Grace of God.

On arrival at the great gatehouse that Monday after Easter, I found the venerable abbey in a state of feverish excitement, with everyone from stable-boys to the abbot greatly focused on what might be uncovered during the excavations to be launched the following day. Few, if any, slept an undisturbed night, and faces looked excited and animated at the usually tranquil and languid office of Vigils in the small hours of the watch. From the opening invocation, "*Lord open thou my lips, and my mouth shall proclaim your praise*", there was a mood of expectancy, and I caught it,

although was troubled that some of my sleepless-
ness came not from excitement, but also from an
unexpected sense of foreboding that I could not
as yet identify.

When the abbey bell rang again shortly before dawn, I once more made my way through
the cold darkness to the scarred church, where I
was joined by those several sisters who had accompanied me from Shaftesbury and, together
with the good brothers, we celebrated Lauds,
Prime, and Mass. When we had finished giving
praise and the servers had cleared the altar, Abbot
Henry directed all to assemble in the gardens.

The abbey's precincts were expansive and
Brother Gervase, the prior, deployed all able
monks to positions around the grounds, each
with a shovel, spade, pick, mattock, adze, or other
implement for digging. We all sang the *Te deum
laudamus*, then the heavy work of excavation began.

When the abbey's great bells tolled for Terce,
Sext, and None, all those directly involved in the
physical endeavours were excused attendance in
church, while the less able monks and guests re-
paired to the choir stalls and sang the offices of

the *opus dei* for the salvation of everyone's souls, as the Psalmist commanded *seven times a day I shall praise you because of your righteous judgments.*

The digging was arduous in the still-hard earth and, after Sext, the kitchens produced bread, cheese, and a broth of leeks and herbs for all, but without disturbing the work, which continued apace. Despite the passing hours, the mood of all did not pall but, if anything, grew ever more feverish. Two cries went up during the day but, to everyone's intense disappointment, the first turned out merely to herald the discovery of a large dressed stone, almost certainly left over from the extensive building work at the abbey after the conquest. The second also turned out to be a disappointment, when it was discovered to be the remains of an ancient well, now dry.

Despite the general mood of excitement, my sense of disquiet had hardened into an inexplicable dread that would not leave me. I have at times in my life found I have a preternatural sense of things, which I have put down to the potent mixture of a voluble nature and the Spirit occasionally granting me some glimpses of *what is and what is to be*, but for what purpose I know not. On this occasion, however, my sense of ill-portent was a mystery to me, and not improved by the appearance of two outsized, night-black ravens settling on the roof of the abbey church and remaining there for hours, their heads flicking back and forth as they took in the scene. I was familiar with the sagas, and knew of dread Odin, the All-Father, worshipped for centuries in this land as the overlord of all and of the dead at Valhalla. He was a fearsome being, who had plucked out one of his eyes to cast into Mimir's Well for the gift of knowledge, impaled himself on the dwarves' great spear Gungnir, then sacrificed himself to himself for nine days on Yggdrasil, the world tree. He was also the master of two formidable ravens, Huginn and Munnin, whom he sent out across the earth as his spies. The sight of the two brooding corvids on the church therefore caused me to shudder and, each time I caught sight of them, I turned away with a chill.

Finally, just before the hour to offer Vespers' praises in celebration of lighting the lamps, there was a tumult a few yards from the cloister. The entire abbey quickly became apprised of it, and all diggers hurried with their tools to join the onlookers at the source of the cries.

As soon as I got to the area, it was immediately clear what was generating the commotion. There, exposed by the perspiring and exhausted excavators, was the unmistakable form of a pyramid buried about a forearm's length beneath the grass.

Without delay Prior Gervase deployed the other diggers to assist in uncovering the pyramid and, within the space of half an hour, the stone had been exposed down to its base, and could be reckoned fully the height of a man and a half.

The hunt was now on for the second pyramid the old bard had described to the lord king Henry, and it was soon discovered some distance to the south of the first. As the excavation continued, accompanied by the uncontrolled excitement of all present, the diggers soon uncovered a weighty stone slab lying between the two pyramids. When the soil was carefully removed from its surface, there was revealed a lead panel in the shape of a cross affixed to it, and on it an inscription. Water was poured on to cleanse it, and the words then appeared as clearly as the day they had been hammered in. I could make them out without assistance, and this is what they said: "Here in the Isle of Avalon lies buried the renowned King Arthur with Winneveria his second wife".

When the panel and stone slab were both lifted, underneath was revealed a large section of old tree trunk, neatly cut and shaped, at least four feet in width and seven in length. Being in such proximity to the cloister, it was immediately apparent that the trunk lay in a north-south orientation, and I drew this to Abbot Henry's attention, informing him that this was common among the ancient pagan burials of the region, but unheard of as a Christian practice. The good abbot was a learned man, and he understood my anxiety immediately. His broad, dark blond brows wrinkled, and his ever-perceptive, green eyes moved quickly as he admitted he could not explain what lay before us. I confess that the sight of it did nothing to quell my deepening feelings of anxiety.

At the request of Prior Gervase, Brother Walter, the abbey's carpenter, climbed down into the excavation trench and began examining the tree trunk. After inspecting it from every angle he declared it to be hollow, constructed of a base and a lid, with the two joined together by wooden plugs and a seal of tar. He promptly ordered his novices to fetch certain tools from his workshop and, before long, they returned bearing the requested implements. After working with the tools for some while on the join between the two halves, Brother Walter called for a number of brothers to attach stout ropes, and we all then heard the tomb's ancient seal cracking open as they pulled off the uppermost half of the arboreal sarcophagus.

For you are dust, and to dust you shall return, the Scriptures promise, and I had come to know graveyards, not least as abbess of my house of sisters at Shaftesbury. My responsibilities had brought me the knowledge that after a body has been several decades in the ground awaiting the Resurrection, only the bones remain. And thereafter Providence turns some bones to dust in several years, while others may take centuries to crumble to nothingness. In cold, damp climes like the west of England, bones do not remain in the earth for long, but are soon pulverized. I was therefore expecting the hollow within the tree tomb to contain mounds of royal dust, with perhaps some small remnant of one or two of the more substantial limbs like a hip or thigh bone. Beyond the excitement of the mortal remains, I was, however, principally hoping that maybe the regal couple had been laid to rest with some ancient jewels, coins, weapons, instruments, or other objects of interest.

Instead, when the upper portion of the sarcophagus was moved away, the vision that greeted us was more hellish than anything I have perceived when afflicted by fever in the blackness of the night. I closed my eyes in revulsion at the sight, and instinctively crossed myself three times, shuddering to the depths of my being.

The royal couple were supine, laid out side-by-side. He was physically imposing: broad, and easily a head taller than most men. She also was tall, with a noticeably slender frame. But the cause of the audible gasps of horror among the onlookers — some of whom had recoiled at the abomination — was that where the intervening centuries should have taken away all clothes and flesh, they had done so only in part.

The annals are filled with the holiest of saints, like Cuthbert, Æthelthryth, and Ælfheah, whose bodies were integrally preserved by the Spirit uncorrupted after death. But what I beheld in the cold earth at Glastonbury was not the repose of the blessed. Rather, it was an unutterable blasphemy and a sin against the Spirit.

The royal couple's mortal remains appeared hideously half-dead. Clumps of rancid flesh, partial organs, and flaps of skin hung onto sections of their skeletons, while in other areas slimy, browned bones were fully exposed. Their mouths still held several teeth, and both scalps sprouted tufts and hanks of rotted hair. The king's was a dirty acorn colour, as were the patchy remnants of beard protruding off his jaw, while on the queen the mangy tresses clinging to sections of scalp were of an anaemic red. Their clothes, too, which the grave should have swallowed, clung in decomposing tatters about them. He also bore sections of corroded chainmail, in areas stuck to bone where there was no muscle or sinew to support it. Similarly, rags of dull, mouldy blue lapped around her, with occasional hints of dulled gold thread just visible in the gathering twilight.

The pair of putrid cadavers was an abomination not of this world, or the next. It was neither life nor death, purgatory nor hell, but some other hideous state of which the Scriptures do not speak. Some of the onlookers averted their eyes and groaned in revulsion. I heard a voice intoning the words of the Psalmist, "*For though I walk through the valley of the shadow of death, I shall fear no evil, for you are with me, your rod and staff comfort me*".

Barely had this horror registered with the crowd than another, even greater, manifested itself. I still shudder as I recollect it, and struggle to find the words to capture the sheer terror that seized all present. Never had the depredations of the Danish heathens on our holy places or the assaults of the Saracens on the land where His feet trod caused blood to turn cold so instantly, for the feculent remnants of one of the eye orbs in the hideous half-thing that once had been Guinevere slowly rolled towards the onlookers. My heart stopped beating for what seemed an age. Some screamed and fled, but I found myself unable to tear my gaze from that hideous jelly. However, the paralysis passed when I eventually appreciated that the foul eye was again still, and I reasoned that it must merely have been resettling after being disturbed by the removal of the tree-tomb's lid.

The ungodly horror of the rotting cadavers still froze the air, and Abbot Henry swiftly approached the graveside to recite a prayer of blessing over the foul remains. Ashen-faced, and with his leonine features set in grim solemnity, he commanded that the planned ceremony be commenced, and so a two-person litter that had been dressed with sumptuous cushions and regal blue damask was brought forward. The bodies were carefully lifted and laid onto it, and a solemn procession to the abbey church began. This cortège was led by a crucifer holding aloft a large ceremonial crucifix, four lucifers with tall, white candles at each corner of the litter, and thurifers at the front and back, wreathing the bier in fumes of sweet frankincense and spices. All followed, singing the *Confitebor* in solemn unison, "*I will give thanks to you, O Lord, with all my heart . . . all the kings of the earth will give you thanks*".

The procession passed the cloisters, then moved down the south side of the great abbey church towards the grand west entrance. As the litter was on the verge of entering into the cool shade of the temple, I found myself unexpectedly praying that some divine force would prevent the progress of that hellish procession, but no heavenly intervention came. The monks were now singing the forty-third psalm, "*I will enter unto the altar of the Lord*", and the litter passed through the tall, arched doorway into the pristine, new Lady Chapel, and then on into the holy temple's long nave.

When it was my turn to enter the great doorway, I could see that up ahead the litter had already reached a point under the ravaged stone rood screen, with its large effigies of Christ flanked by Saints Peter and Paul looking down on the calm scene below. The procession moved on, and the royal couple were soon at the high altar, where they were laid onto an ornamental catafalque set out in readiness to receive their earthly remains.

The lucifers stationed themselves at the four sides of the royal display, pointing outwards to the cardinal points of the compass, and we all filed solemnly around the bodies, praying for the repose of their eternal souls. As I gazed upon the hideous countenances, the feeling of dread that had been with me since the previous evening now crystallized into a certainty that, in unearthing these monstrosities, we had brought something beyond God's law into the abbey.

Some of the brothers remained to sing a belated Vespers, but I excused myself and made my way through the gloom to the tranquility of the abbey's ancient library where, in the shade of its cool arches, I located Nennius's *Historia brittonum* among the presses piled high with the brothers' famed collection of volumes. The light was poor and no candle was permitted in that shrine to the written word, but my eyes were still young enough to read in the penumbra.

I had recalled that Nennius's account of Arthur related that he was a most pious Christian, and I soon found the passage affirming that Arthur was so strong in the faith that he carried an image of the Blessed Mary Ever Virgin into the Battle of Guinnion Castle. While pleased that my memory had not deceived me, this confirmation meant that the monstrous burial uncovered that afternoon was a grotesque perversion of the grace and faith that had illuminated Arthur's life.

As I read further into Nennius's deeds of Arthur, two other episodes I had not recalled now stood out and troubled me. One recorded that in the region of Buelt, Arthur's dog, Cabal, had left the imprint of his paw on a stone. Arthur piled up a mound of rocks and placed the imprinted stone on top, but if ever anyone carried it away, the following morning it was always again atop the pile. This was, I reflected, not like one of the glorious saints' miracles that testify to the majesty of God, but more akin to pagan magic that served no purpose other than to glorify its spell-weaver.

The other told of a grave at Ergyng in which lay Anir, Arthur's son, whom Arthur slew and buried there. The grave was plainly cursed, as whosoever measured it arrived at a different size each time — perhaps six, nine, twelve, or fifteen feet long and wide — and the measurement was never twice the same. This, too, I shuddered, was not a godly miracle, as it served no benevolent or salvific purpose. It was something other. Something dark.

Filled with disquiet, I scoured the deserted library, and eventually located another book I wanted to consult, Geoffrey of Monmouth's compendious *Historia regum britannie*, in which I was able to refresh my mind on the history of the wild-man and sorcerer Merlin, whose dark magic had always troubled me, seeming to have no place in the most Christian age of Arthur.

I reread in Geoffrey how the unfortunate Vortigern, king of Britain, had been chased into

Wales by an army of invading Anglo-Saxons. Once deep into that country, he endeavoured to construct a strong. defensive tower, but the masonry kept falling in, so he summoned magicians to advise him. They inspected the site, and ordered that a fatherless youth be brought and sacrificed so that the tower's foundation stones could be bathed in blood and thereby cemented together. A suitable youth was soon located — the son of a nun who had been ravished by a beautiful daemonic incubus — and the boy was brought to the tower. Before being slain, however, the victim disclosed to King Vortigern that there was a pond under the tower in which two dragons were locked in mortal combat. One was red, he explained, and represented the British people, while the other was white, and symbolized the Germanic invaders. Vortigern duly ordered the pond uncovered and drained, and the two dragons were exposed for all to see. The youth who had told these wondrous things to Vortigern was Merlin, whose powers were recognized that day, and so Vortigern spared his life. Once grown to adulthood, Merlin was sent to Ireland with King Uther Pendragon, where he used a great feat of magic to transport the Giants' Dance ring of standing stones to the plain near Salisbury. And finally, not long after, Uther found himself unable to concentrate or sleep for lust of Igraine of Tintagel, wife of Gorlois, one of his most loyal retainers. Uther therefore demanded Merlin's magical assistance, whereupon Merlin transformed Uther into the physical likeness of Gorlois. Uther thus deceived Igraine into lying with him, and she thereby conceived a child, whom she named Arthur. Such was the tale of Merlin I found in Geoffrey of Monmouth's chronicle, and I closed the book, shuddering inwardly. They were but legends, old tales of the countryside, but yet something in what I had seen that afternoon in the exhumation of the two cadavers gave me pause for thought.

I put the old volumes away, and retired to the guesthouse. I had no appetite for the evening's collation, and slept fitfully, missing the day's final prayers at Compline, disturbed by feverish dreams of Arthur and Guinevere's foul cadavers. I placed myself into God's hands and prayed the words of the Scripture, *When you lie down, you will not be afraid. For you will lie down, and your sleep will be sweet.* But repose was denied me.

Unable to rest properly, I prayed from my book of hours and, when the abbey was dark and silent, lit a candle and made my way down to the church, having resolved to continue my prayers over the corpses to mediate for the ongoing repose of their souls. Something in my gnawing sense of dread had convinced me that their immortal essences were not at peace. And also, I knew, I wished to allay my fears that something terrible would be the result of our actions that day. Time alone in the church, I hoped, would help calm me, as holy spaces invariably do.

When I entered the shattered building, the cool nave was quiet and smelled heavily of the incense that had impregnated the stones' pores for centuries. There was no one about at this hour, and — despite the visible charring and scarring all around — I nevertheless felt the still of the great building settle over me, as if I were in the womb of a vast stony dragon. I lit several candles at the chancel, and lay face-down on the floor, my arms spread as if being crucified alongside Our Lord. I then began my orisons, every now and then glancing up at the ghastly bodies on the catafalque, trying to imagine them at peace with the saints. As I became more used to them, a calmness gently began to enfold me.

I was just gathering into my thoughts all those souls waiting in the hope of the everlasting Resurrection when, quite unexpectedly, my insides clenched violently, freezing instantly to ice. For a moment I was terrified, wondering if I had been *smitten with madness and blindness and bewilderment of mind* for my failure to understand the word of God. But I just as quickly understood I was not dying, rather that my body was reacting to a danger it had sensed but my eyes had not yet seen. Then, in an instant, I did see.

At first the motion was so slow as to be indiscernible, and I reassured myself it was no more than the movement of shadows cast by the tall candles' flickering flames. And then I hoped that it was no more than that sometimes we confuse the wanderings of the mind with reality. But, in another instant, there was no doubt, and I was somehow on my feet, animated by an existential terror that could not have been greater if all purgatory's tortures had been unveiled to me at once.

Guinevere's cadaver was moving.

Sensing the icy hand around my viscera

clenching tighter, I lurched to escape whatever it was rising off the catafalque, but — like Lot's wife fleeing Sodom and Gomorrah — I was rooted to the floor like a pillar of salt as I beheld Guinevere slowly raise her torso and sit upright.

A scream that seemed to come from my throat — although not at my command — broke the spell, and my previously paralyzed legs were now pumping beneath me. Before I knew it, I had hurtled half way down the choir in the direction of the door leading out to the cloister. As I fled, the sound of my shoes on the stone flags thundered in my ears, and then I heard an impossibility that I still struggle to bring myself to describe, but it was the sure sound of footfalls ringing out in the silence behind me. My terror knew no bounds, and then another sound I had not even contemplated caused me, I think, to blank out for a moment, yet still I kept running. It was the unmistakable rhythm of a second set of footsteps pursuing me.

I could not resist the instinct to turn and look, and I almost toppled over as the sight stilled my blood to the quick. Both Guinevere and Arthur were about twenty yards behind me in the gloom, advancing at a preternatural speed that was not of this world. His skeletal face burned with the malignity of *the father of lies*, while hers exuded all the heat and rage of *the fire of Gehenna*.

I grasped the large, jewel-studded, pectoral cross of my abbess's office about my neck, and held it out towards the daemons, all the while still fleeing uncontrollably for my life. I commanded, "Be Gone in the name of Christ!" invoking the many exorcisms Our Lord performed, but neither cross nor invocations had any effect. The fiends were now only five yards behind me, and I could see flecks of saliva on Arthur's decomposing lips flying off as his head shook with each of his powerful footfalls.

Before I knew it, I was at the north wall and seizing the ceramic stoup of holy water from the lavabo niche. I hurled it at the apparitions as my shoulder hit the door out into the cloister, and I was through it. I heard the earthenware strike one of them, and anticipated the footsteps would stop with a scream of defiant pain and rage. But, to my incomprehension and horror, the potent, blessed water had no effect, and still I heard the footsteps closing on me.

I slammed the great door, yet my state was such that I fumbled the bolt and had to push it across a second time, hearing it bang noisily into place only a fraction of a moment before the two infernal bodies collided with its heavy, gnarled oak. I did not stop running, and the sound of the ghouls repeatedly smashing into the door behind me only impelled my legs all the faster.

I was insensible with terror and, without any conscious thought, found myself tearing open the door of Abbot Henry's dayrooms, bursting in with no idea how I had arrived there. I no longer recall what I frenziedly relayed to the abbot and Gerald, who were in the midst of an earnesr discussion but, in no time, Henry was hurriedly leading us both up a flight of stairs back towards the abbey church.

I must have refused to return there because I remember the good abbot reassuring me that no harm would come to us. At first I assumed he meant he could take on these infernal daemons himself, as he was powerfully built, with broad shoulders and firm legs, a physique which had gained him a reputation as an athlete and horseman. But within a few moments I understood, as he led us into a blind corridor. Once approaching its dead end, he indicated two large slits in the stonework akin to loopholes in a castle wall and, in no time, we were upon them, peering down into the abbey church from the level of its first-floor triforium.

I could hear what sounded like Arthur and Guinevere's steps echoing in the church's cavernous space but, when I scanned the abbey's floor, I saw nothing. I struggled to understand how my ears were hearing their shouts but my eyes could not see them, yet all the while the fiends were screeching what seemed like recriminations at each other. I could understand nothing of their invective in what sounded like the old Brittonic tongue, but Gerald could, as it remains the language of his native country.

"He blames Guinevere," Gerald whispered haltingly. "For bringing down the kingdom —". The priest's breathing was ragged. "For her love for Lancelot, which poisoned the court and turned sworn friends one against the other." Gerald's thin frame shook as he spoke, his sallow, emaciated face gaunt and pale.

I was scanning the church floor below, peering at the patchwork of exquisite multicoloured tiling interspersed with areas of devastation where the flames had left nothing but scorched earth, when my eye was caught by a movement opposite, and I raised my gaze to the far wall of the nave, where some patches still bore traces of paint amid the charred and blackened sections.

The sight that greeted me caused my knees to buckle, and Abbot Henry put out a firm, steadying arm to support me as I pointed mutely through the aperture at what my understanding of Creation was not able to comprehend.

Arthur and Guinevere were scuttling across the vertical wall, on all fours, like large, rotting beetles. They were high up, at the level of the second storey, moving at great speed, defying all laws of nature. As I watched, Arthur pounced on Guinevere, who screamed as he hammered a blow into her abdomen where her solar plexus would have been. The force of the impact detached her body from the wall, and she hung in mid-air for a moment, before plummeting to the ground.

I assumed the savagery of the blow would have shattered her ribcage. And likewise the impact onto the hard floor to have smashed her into many shards. But Guinevere lay spread out on the flags, in one piece, and entirely still.

In an instant Arthur had scrambled headfirst down the wall, and was beside her at the foot of one of the four large candelabra that screened off the high altar steps. Moving purposefully, he ripped off one of the great silver chains that ran between the candelabra bases, and used it roughly to bind Guinevere's arms and legs to her body. By now she was shouting again with all the venom of centuries of seething rage. Unperturbed, Arthur left her bound on the nave floor, and moved up to the high altar.

"She is accusing him of being no man," Gerald continued. "That he is nothing without Merlin's spells. That he is weak, like his father, Uther, who could not win Igraine of Tintagel's heart, so satisfied his lust by violating her using the deceit of Merlin's foul conjurations, creating Arthur as their hell-spawned bastard."

"God save us," Abbot Henry interrupted, pointing towards the high altar, where I saw nothing at first, but then slowly discerned a collection of dark shapes. They had a nebulous quality, like puffs of smoke but, as we watched in fascination and horror, they started to coalesce into separate forms and, even before I had finished counting,

I know how many there would be. A paralysis took hold of me as I confirmed that there were exactly eleven. Together with Arthur, that made twelve. The fraternity of the Round Table, now returned from hell. As they took shape out of the smoke, it was plain that they, too, like Arthur and Guinevere, were half-decayed corpses, covered in a ragged and rotting assortment of flesh, clothes, armour, and weapons.

"Make haste!" Abbot Henry was already running back down the corridor. "We must gather everyone in the cellars."

The abbot rushed to the main dormitory, and I ran to the guesthouse, where the small party of sisters that had accompanied me from Shaftesbury was lodging alongside me. I mustered and conveyed them to the cellars, ignoring their various questions about what was amiss. In truth, I knew not how to relay to them what I had seen.

Roused form their sleep in the dormitory, the monks were already assembling in the undercrofts, where Abbot Henry appointed Prior Gervase and several others from among the more senior brothers to ensure everyone was brought there, and that the cellar's sturdy doors were firmly secured and bolted. The abbot, Gerald, and I then set off again, this time to find those who spent the nights elsewhere, mainly grooms, stable-lads, cooks, gardeners, masons, and all the others who kept the abbey fed, working, and in good repair.

"First, Brother Vitalis," the abbot shouted, making for the church. "In the belltower."

Gerald and I followed as Henry led us into the cloister, up the stairs to the first-floor dormitory that had just been evacuated, and then to the small, night-door leading from the dormitory into the church that served the monks for attending the night and morning offices.

"It's the only way," Henry explained, pushing the door, which opened onto an arcaded passageway running down the church's first-floor triforium. "There's a staircase at the end leading into the belltower."

The prospect of entering the building wherein were the chthonic beings we had seen earlier caused every fibre of my being to rebel, but Abbot Henry was already through the door and onto the balcony and, without time to demur, Gerald and I followed him onto the dilapidated walkway, and I immediately spied the belltower staircase around ten yards ahead.

Moving speedily along the rubble-strewn corridor, curiosity got the better of me, and I peered down into the broken church below, to be greeted by a sight that remains seared into my mind, and which I see again before me now as vividly as if I was beholding the abominable scene afresh.

Guinevere and one of the wraith knights were lashed together in an embrace, secured by yet more silver chains ripped from the candelabra. Thus trussed up, they had been suspended from the rood screen using another silver chain thrown over the partition's central arcade. Whether through anger or fear I could not tell, but the pair were shouting monstrously as they swung above a fire being stoked by a small party of rotting knights. Smoke was rising and, as I gazed on that hellish scene, I saw the flames begin to lap at the couple's feet. Their frenzied shouts now echoed ceaselessly around the ancient stone walls, mingled with the hideous, gleeful cheers of their tormentors.

I found myself rooted to the spot by the ghastliness of the scene, paralyzed by revulsion at the spectacle of the flames catching the packets of flesh on the couple's legs, before Guinevere's clothes erupted into a fireball. As if in obscene mockery, the rood's effigies of Christ, Saints Peter and Paul looked benignly down onto the depraved scene, oblivious to the blasphemy being enacted.

In no time, Guinevere and her companion were invisible inside a raging conflagration, the fat in their flesh and hair feeding the hungry flames, infusing the air of that sacred place with the odours of scorched meat. Bile was rising in my throat, and I clamped my eyes closed, straining to recall the serenity of my flower garden at Shaftesbury, struggling to conjure to my mind its carnations, lilies, roses, and violets, craving to infuse my nostrils with memories of their sweet perfumes. But instead my mind turned of its own volition to that ghastly commandment of the Apostle, wherein he instructed the faithful to deliver immoral sinners *to Satan for the destruction of the flesh, that the spirit may be saved in the day of the Lord Jesus.* I had never before seen a burning in obedience to this commandment as they are not part of the English tradition, and I felt a wave of hot nausea at the thought the Scriptures could license scenes as abominable as the one before me.

There was a rough tug at my arm, and Gerald was hauling me towards the belltower staircase with a strength I had not expected from such a thin-framed, bookish man. In a moment we were on the first step, and running up the narrow stone spiral to the bell chamber. Arriving breathless at the top, we spied in the gloom an elderly, hollow-faced and bearded monk resting on a small pallet beside a water clock. He awoke at the unexpected intrusion, and gazed at us in bewilderment.

Abbot Henry commanded him to leave his post at once and follow us, but Brother Vitalis replied that he had rung the Vigils bell for four decades, and would do so again that night. The abbot remonstrated with him, but Vitalis remained intractable. In desperation, the abbot hurled all manner of dire warnings at the elderly monk, before disclosing what was occurring in the church below. Contrary to the abbot's intention, this fresh information rendered Vitalis even more obdurate, now asserting that he would stand guard and instead ring the bells as an alarm to warn the neighbourhood if the fiends began escaping. "*For so the Lord said to me,*" he avowed with finality. "*Go, set a watchman, let him declare what he sees.*"

Defeated, and reminding us all that precious seconds were slipping away, the abbot led us back down the steps and again onto the broken triforium gallery passage. Once more I could not prevent myself glancing down into the church below, where I saw that the hellish scene was still before me, but Guinevere and her companion were no longer recognizable. Everything of them had been burnt away, leaving just the bones, a few patches of mail on the knight, and some rings on Guinevere's bony fingers. Their skeletons were now fully blackened and the flames had retreated, yet still they danced remorselessly under them. From the captives' vigorous shouts, the immolation had not subdued them and, at that moment, I understood that what was already dead could not die. More terrifying than this discovery, however, was the realization that — apart from the two burning captives — the abbey church was empty. The ghoul Arthur and his ten daemonic knights were now at large in the abbey.

In no time we were in the dormitory and then back at ground level in the cloisters, where we grouped in the southwest corner. I was struggling to make sense of what was happening. It was too much for a sane mind to bear and. in that moment, as I gulped down deep, vast, lungsful of cold night air, something in me broke. The visceral fear and horror I had been feeling were both suddenly pushed into the background, and my predominant emotion became a volcanic anger. The desecration of God's holy house by the fiends had pushed me close to the edge. But it was their greater blasphemy that now filled me with rage: the desecration of the love between Guinevere and Lancelot, for it could only be he chained to her. Theirs was not a love sanctioned by sacrament to bring two together like Christ and his bridal Church, but it was a love God had undoubtedly kindled in them — for all love is of God — and to see them immolated for it, in a church, a temple of divine love, was too much for me to countenance. It was a crime against the fabric of the universe for, without love, there is nothing, *and the fate of man and of beasts is the same, as one dies, so dies the other and they all have the same breath, and man has no advantage over the beasts, for all is vanity*. At this realization an idea that been inchoately forming began to take firmer shape in my mind.

"This necromancy is the Devil's work," Gerald interrupted my thoughts, gasping and shaking visibly.

"If it were of the Devil," I countered, "it could not thrive in the house of God, *for the dragon was cast out, that serpent of old*, and has no way back into God's grace, into his house. Whatever it is in there," and I knew I was right, "lies beyond the Devil, and beyond our understanding."

Gerald wrestled with my words for a few moments, his expression reflecting an inner turmoil. Then his shoulders hunched and his face drained of all residual colour. "So, we are lost."

I shook my head. "The dead do not rise," I ventured, "unless by the power of Heaven, as Elijah and Elisha commanded of old, as Our Lord ordered of the son of the widow of Nain, Jairus's daughter, and Lazarus, as Peter commanded of Tabitha, and as Paul demanded of Eutychus. Yet nowhere do the Scriptures hold any example of the Devil reanimating the dead, for his power is death, not life." In as much as it terrified me, I could not avoid the conclusion I was reaching. "This is not of God, or the Devil. It is other."

"What else can there be?" Abbot Henry interjected, his tone a mixture of fear and exasperation. "The masters of Oxford, Paris, and Bologna have stated many times that all which is outside Scripture is superstition and to be given no credence."

"And yet," my confidence in my conclusion was absolute, "they have not seen what we have. This can only be the old magic of the forests, of the druids, and of the arch-druid, Merlin. It has its own ways and rhythms of which we know nothing. It is the power of nature from primitive times. It is oblivious to our Scriptures and sacraments. And our sacraments know nothing of it."

"Then, what weapons — " Abbot Henry began, but I was ahead of him.

"Send for your brother apothecary," I ordered.

"He will have no salves or balms — " the abbot began, but I cut him short.

"With haste, my lord abbot," I instructed.

Saying nothing further, the abbot disappeared towards the conventual buildings, leaving Gerald and me alone. The cloisters were deserted and, as we stood in silence, we heard only the wind. My racing heart was calmer now, and I looked out over the dilapidated quadrangle's roof to the church and belltower, and screamed.

Brother Vitalis was standing in the opening on the near side of the belltower, but behind him was the unmistakable glint of a fast-moving strip of metal flashing in the moonlight. And then it was done and I felt the bile rise in my gorge as the blade passed fully through the elderly monk's neck. His body toppled forwards and, as it did, the head came free of the neck, leaving the stump spouting forth gore as they both fell heavily to earth. The two landed with thuds on the church's roof and, at the same time, one of the hideous creatures scuttled down the outside wall of the belltower, a bloodied sword in hand.

"Make speed!" I grabbed Gerald, and dragged him up the shallow flight of steps into the church.

"Not there!" he recoiled.

I kept firm hold of him. "The ghouls left the church."

We entered the great building, and speedily secreted ourselves behind the large, ancient stone font. Outside, we could hear the fiend's footsteps drawing ever nearer. I do not think I have felt dread like I knew in that moment. I had no skills in defending myself. Gerald had grown up in a castle. but had been educated in the Church his whole life, so knew as little of the practical art of arms as me. If we were discovered, the outcome would not be in question.

In another moment, the footsteps were at the church door. The beast paused and sniffed the air slowly, peering into the gloom. I stopped my breathing and gripped the smooth carvings of the font until my knuckles turned white. After what seemed an age, the ghoul turned away, and headed back down the aisle of the cloister.

As the immediate danger passed, I began shaking, but forced myself to stop the convulsions and wait in the church until Abbot Henry returned, as at least the building offered places to hide.

The time dragged by, but eventually Abbot Henry appeared in the cloister with a lanky, white-haired monk, whose rapid movements suggested a quick, nervous mind. Never had I been so glad to see two faces, and Gerald and I left our hiding place and went out to them.

"*Pax Christi*," the tall man greeted us hurriedly, introducing himself as Brother Anselm.

"Good brother apothecary," I began, with no time for more fulsome formalities. "You travel the roads and villages about the abbey collecting plants, herbs, insects, and other ingredients for your work?"

Anselm nodded.

"On occasion, you purchase items and preparations from local vendors?"

A hint of caution crept into the apothecary's expression. "On occasion," he conceded carefully.

"Be mindful of our Order's oath of obedience," I cautioned him.

He nodded, now with a palpable sense of unease.

"Whatever the fathers teach us of such things, I must ask you, Brother Anselm, have you had dealings with anyone who was apprenticed to the art of the . . . old ways?" I fixed my gaze on him. "You understand me, good brother . . . I am speaking of the forest ways?"

The tall monk shot the abbot an apprehensive glance.

"In your estimation," I continued, "might any of them have a reputation as being gifted in those ways?"

Anselm spoke carefully. "I was at the exhumation today, and assure you, my lady abbess, nothing that may have occurred here today was on account of anything I have brought into the abbey."

"Listen most acutely," I persisted. "There is great danger. Time is short. You must now go to the forest and bring back to me the person there with the greatest skill in the old ways. Our lives — and those of the foresters — very probably depend on it."

Abbot Henry put a hand on the apothecary's shoulder. "With the utmost haste, brother Anselm. We shall await you in the muniments chamber. God speed."

As Anselm's silhouette disappeared into the night, we made for the abbot's dayrooms to which the muniments store was attached. I shall never forget the journey there from the church, hearing the sounds of the beasts ransacking the abbey, while we ran in the shadows, unsure who or what we might meet around each corner.

The muniments room turned out to be a windowless chamber fitted with a solid, lockable door. It was a safe room in which the abbey's most valuable documents were packed into locked chests and, under other circumstances, I would have been delighted to be allowed the freedom of its records, to understand more of that great abbey's past. But on this occasion we sat in the dark, listening out for the scuttling and stamping of the fiends. Several times we heard them nearby, but on no occasion did they sense there was a hidden room. Around us, however, were shouts and occasional screams as they discovered anyone ill-starred enough not to have made it to the security of the abbey's cellars.

We remained there, numb and powerless as the hours passed, until eventually there came an urgent whisper outside the door. Abbot Henry verified it was the apothecary, and we opened the chamber to find Anselm and a second figure, shorter than him, with head and shoulders heavily swathed in a cloak. The five of us then made for the church in haste and silence, this time undisturbed by the sounds of the ghouls, although not without a great trepidation that one or more of them might be lying in wait in the shadows.

Once at the church's great west doorway, Anselm introduced the newcomer. "Wulfrun is the one you seek, my lady abbess." The stranger obliged by removing her hood to reveal a high-cheekboned face probably in its third decade. Even by the weak moonlight I could see she was of uncommonly striking countenance, with a red-purple birthmark underneath one eye, hair the colour of shiny lamp-black, and eyes of pale blue.

I indicated for Wulfrun to look through the church's doorway, and she walked forward to peer into the silent building, taking in the scene of destruction, the fire smouldering on the floor of the nave, and the blackened skeletons of Guinevere and Lancelot swinging above it. They had ceased their shouts, but were still moving their limbs, struggling to be free of the fetters.

When Wulfrun returned to us, there was tension on her face, and it grew more marked as Abbot Henry explained the events of the day. She listened quietly until the end, whereupon he posed the question to which her answer would contain our ruin or salvation.

Her voice was grave in reply. "What you ask is not nothing". She spoke in the English tongue, which we all understood, although used rarely. "And there is always a price." Her voice had a surprising confidence given she was addressing an abbot, abbess, and royal chaplain, whose clothes and jewellery marked us out even in the half-light

"You will be handsomely rewarded," Abbot Henry reassured her.

"I am grateful for whatever you give," she acknowledged. "But I do not speak of payment to me."

"Then what?" Henry regarded her with bewilderment.

"It is not for me to know." There was a surprising directness in her speech again. "Fate will present you with the reckoning. A price will be demanded one day. It will not be trivial, and may even be your life. It will — "

"You dare to address my lord abbot in this way," Gerald rounded on her with indignation.

Wulfrun did not react, but kept her gaze steadily on Henry, who had blanched visibly in the pale moonlight. After a moment, he nodded. "Do what you can."

There was then a silence that seemed to span an aeon, before Wulfrun replied again. "I will need eleven horses."

"The evil number," Gerald crossed himself.

Wulfrun ignored him, and continued. "They will be a . . . gift. By which I mean," she paused, "they will not be returning to the stables."

"This is *maleficium*," Gerald interjected hotly. "My lord abbot, you cannot, in all conscience — "

Henry held up his hand to silence the priest.

"Have them each fitted with a bridle and saddle," Wulfrun continued. "And brought to me here."

The abbot dispatched Anselm to find the head groom and make the necessary preparations.

We all looked to Wulfrun, who raised her hood and obscured her face. "Now I must request you to leave. This work is not for the eyes of the mundane."

"Impossible," Gerald protested angrily. "Under no circumstances would my lord abbot permit a stranger, a woman — "

Wulfrun silenced him with a defiant shake of her head. "Do your Scriptures not say that *your ways are not my ways*? You will have the church back. But now it must be mine."

"We have set out on this path," I affirmed. "There is no gain to be had in bartering over the details."

"So be it," Abbot Henry concluded the discussion.

Wulfrun pointed to a copse of trees several hundred yards off. "Wait among the oaks and hazels. Do not stray. You will know when it is done."

We watched as she entered the church — a small figure in so vast a space, her hood and cloak giving her the outline of a diminutive member of the community from a different age — before she closed the great doors behind her. As we made our way to the trees in silence, I was assailed by a sudden doubt. I had been so certain earlier that summoning one such as Wulfrun was the path we must take. But now, seeing her alone in that enormous place with such evil all about, the idea seemed madness. How could anyone face the beasts we had seen? What had I been thinking to expose someone to such mortal dangers? My proposal had not been fair. How was a simple villager going to refuse the request of so powerful a man as Abbot Henry, whose writ of life and death ran through the countryside for miles around the abbey? It was unprincipled of me to have suggested she be summoned, and her death would be on me as, in all likelihood, we would all be slain, and the hellish creatures would butcher everyone in the abbey before moving beyond its walls and bathing the countryside in blood. On the other hand, even if, by whatever dark imprecations I shuddered to think of, Wulfrun was successful, what sort of malevolent arts would I have unleashed in this most holy of places? It would never be possible to remove the stain of such maleficence from these precincts. Nor — as I was instigatrix of this dark stratagem — from my immortal soul.

We reached the trees and secreted ourselves in them. No-one spoke, and in the cold night air my mind became a vortex of jumbled thoughts. Why had God permitted those abominations into the world, and to cross the sacred threshold of His abbey church? Or — and this idea frightened me as much as the beings themselves — had He been powerless to halt them?

Eventually my reverie was broken by the sound of hooves on the gravel. Although I knew there were only eleven horses, in the darkness they sounded like an army approaching, full of dread purpose. I then saw the church's doors open wide, and the sound of the hooves again, but this time on the solid, cold slabs of the church floor. There was an ominous silence for a short while, then the west doors closed with a muffled bang.

I was assailed by fear. For the fate of the abbey, and for the world if the creatures broke loose. And for the safety of the person about whom we knew nothing, who had shut herself up to do what we, Christ, and the power of England's greatest abbey could not.

The minutes dragged by. None of Abbot Henry, Gerald, or I spoke. It was cold, and I pulled my cloak around me more tightly, wondering what Wulfrun meant when she said we would know when it was done.

There were still periodic noises coming from the abbey buildings, interspersed with the sounds of people in pain. Some of the barns now burned, and the flames were starting to lick high into the sky.

Beside me, I felt Gerald freeze. I turned my gaze slowly in the direction he was looking, and saw two of the abominations running quickly across the grounds. It took me mere moments to draw the same conclusion as Gerald. They were making directly for us. The Easter moon was bright, and I could clearly make out that they had their decrepit yet still lethal weapons drawn, and were approaching fast.

I expected to feel fear but, for some strange reason, a calm purpose settled over me, along with a surprising and violent, almost elated, urge to batter these apparitions into the ground if they came any closer. It was not a feeling I have experienced before or since, and I can only assume it was something that lies deep within — like the murderous rage of Samson pulling down the temple of Dagon on the Philistines — ready to be roused when no other options remain.

Within moments, the fiends were upon us, and the foulness of their decomposition and bodily corruption rendered me ever more enraged. I howled at them in defiance, while Abbot Henry and Gerald cast about for anything to serve us as weapons.

My rage and sense of cold, violent purpose were then joined by an intense feeling of claustrophobia. I wondered if this was part of feeling the very end approaching, and I shivered at the prospect of the cold steel slicing into me. But then I knew that the claustrophobia was truly physical, as the space in which we were standing had somehow become smaller. And it was continuing to shrink.

At this sudden feeling of being penned in, I looked to my left and right to see what was happening, only to discover that the branches of the trees had moved downwards and inwards, and were now forming a thick, defensive wall around us. My mind wrestled with this impossibility of nature, yet I clearly saw the boughs continue to move, until there were several yards of thick, protective canopy all round us, reaching down to the ground, surrounding and shielding us on all sides. At this miracle, the Scriptures came to my mind. *The branch of the Lord will be beautiful and glorious . . . It will be a shelter and shade from the heat of the day, and a refuge and hiding place from the storm and rain.* But I knew it was not the Lord who had commanded the trees. It was Wulfrun's bidding.

I could hear the ghouls howling in frustration as they tried to get at us, but with every thrust of their rusty blades the trees pressed in closer, and we were as untouchable and secure as if in a stone tower. I recall thinking triumphantly, *With great delight I sat in his shadow, and his fruit was sweet to my taste,* but I fear I was becoming delirious. Eventually the sounds of the fiends quietened, and finally ceased completely. After a few more moments the boughs slowly lifted, and the hellhounds were gone.

Still none of us spoke, perhaps not willing to admit what we had all just experienced. But, before the silence became awkward, the temperature of the air plummeted, and my ears filled with a great sound that stopped the blood in my veins. It was neither a moan, sigh, nor scream, but a chilling combination of all three, seemingly rising up from the earth out of the throats of the beasts of the infernal, sulphurous depths. At the same moment I saw, through the abbey church's few remaining windows, that the candles which burned day and night on the altars and shrines were all at once extinguished. Then the west doors blew open with a deafening din, and a great wind rushed forth out of the building. At the same time I perceived a swirling haze of what seemed like iridescent dust bursting out of the arched doorway. It seemed to reach up several storeys, and in it I clearly discerned the nightmarish, distorted, billowing faces of horses and riders as the cloud swelled with a thunderous noise to an impossible size. And then it was gone, evaporated into the air. As quickly as it had become icy cold and the dust cloud had appeared, the temperature returned to normal, and there was only the stillness and wind of the April evening.

Without saying a word, all three of us ran to the west entrance. Abbot Henry was through first, then Gerald, and me last. Inside it was dark, but moonlight streamed through the doorway and the windows, illuminating the unspeakable scene before us.

The eleven horses were tethered to the great, ancient font by the west door, arrayed around it in a circle. They all lay on the floor, dead, while the font's immense bowl glistened black with blood from their opened throats. On the saddle of each was a rider, now a browned dry skeleton, shorn of all the scraps of flesh and hair and apparel that had until so recently clung to the half-dead monstrosities. God forgive me for what Wulfrun had unleashed in His house, but I breathed a sigh of profound relief from the depth of my soul at the sight of the eleven malevolent knights lying inert like stone effigies of the horsemen of the Apocalypse.

Wulfrun's face, arms, and clothing were stained with blood, and she was moving among the horses, closing the dead eyelids over their large, still eyes. As my sight accustomed to the gloom, I saw over by the rood screen that the charred bones of Guinevere and Lancelot still hung under it. And, with a jolt of horror, I realized that the two were still moving.

Wulfrun observed my reaction. "The horses have taken their riders to the next world. Forever. But the Lord and the Lady have other plans for them." She indicated the two now clamouring to be freed.

"In the abbey graveyard there is a pit freshly dug with a blank headstone." She was now addressing the abbot and Gerald. "Take these two down and place them in that grave."

"It has just been cut for Brother Ranulf," the abbot protested. "He was gathered unto God yesterday, and — "

Wulfrun cut him off. "His interment can wait." She led them to Guinevere and Lancelot. "It must be done. Now."

"But they're — " Gerald began.

Wulfrun shook her head. "Neither are they dead. Now do as I ask."

The abbot and Gerald released the chain keeping the skeletons suspended in the air, and

lowered them to the ground. The pair were writh-
ing to be freed and crying out horribly, but Henry
and Gerald lifted them up and carried the couple
out into the night. A while later, they returned,
streaked with dirt, and confirmed they had placed
the bones in the grave before filling it over with
earth.

"One final task," Wulfrun announced, moving over to the chapel of the Holy Thorn, taking
up a large sprig of the spiky plant that still grew
on Wearyall Hill where St Joseph had planted it,
then bringing it back to us.

She approached me and, taking hold of my
thumb, pressed it firmly onto one of the twig's
spiky thorns, drawing blood. Her grip was firm,
and I did not flinch, but let the crimson drops
stain the stem.

"Now a man," she looked about, withdraw-
ing the spike from my thumb.

Seeing my gaze flit to Abbot Henry, she approached him, then performed the same exercise
with his thumb, but on a different part of the
thorn branch. As she did so, I thought I heard her
breathe the words "*hoc est conjunctionem opposi-
torum*" as thick gouts of his blood began to drip

down onto the thin, green twig. But I assumed I was mistaken, as I could not conceive how a person from the forest could know of the ancient philosophic wisdom of Anaximander. And yet, maybe I had heard correctly, as clearly the arts she had deployed that evening had their roots in an ancient well.

When Wulfrun was finished, she tucked the thorn into a small pouch on her belt. "I will need two cups of wine and two small, sweet cakes."

The abbot nodded.

"Have someone bring them to me in the graveyard."

We followed Wulfrun out of the abbey church. "Burn the horses and riders so hot they turn to dust," she added. "And do not consume any of the horse meat or use any part of them for any purpose."

We stopped when we arrived at the arched and gated entrance to the graveyard.

"Brother Anselm will see that the abbey furnishes you and your family with all you will ever need," Abbot Henry informed Wulfrun, his business-like tone not quite masking the palpable gratitude in his voice. "But there is no amount of money, clothing, and food that can reflect what you have done tonight. How can we ever thank you adequately?"

"By giving me peace now." Her hand was on the gate's latch. "And by paying the Lord and Lady, when the price is asked."

The abbot nodded almost imperceptibly, then looked towards the freshly covered grave. "And what of — " he paused. "Will they — ?"

Wulfrun shook her head. "They will not bother you again."

"Then," Abbot Henry concluded, "I give you the peace of Christ."

The look that stole across Wulfrun's face seemed to indicate that she marvelled at the abbot's ongoing trust in the power of Christ after what had transpired that evening, but it was followed by a sincere and tired smile. With that, she was gone through the gate into the graveyard.

As the three of us walked away, I took my leave. I was exhausted, and wanted nothing more than to be alone in my room, and to start the lifelong process of trying to understand what God had shown me that evening.

I wearily climbed the stairs of the guesthouse and found my chambers. Once inside, I closed its door and leant heavily against it for a moment, keeping all I had seen outside. The window was open, and I went over to it to inhale the cool evening air. As I did, I noticed the graveyard was clearly illuminated in the moonlight. Wulfrun was beside the new grave. And I could see that on it she had placed the bloodied Holy Thorn, the two cups of wine, and the two sweet cakes.

I watched for an age. Wulfrun did not move and, although I could see her lips forming words, she was too far away for me to hear what they were. My eyelids grew heavy as I gazed at her, transfixed, until eventually tiredness overtook me.

I slipped off my shoes and habit and put on my nightshift. There was a bowl of cold water on a stand, and I washed my face and rubbed my teeth with the soft stick and ground cloves and herbs that had been left out for me. Before climbing into bed, I took one final look out of the window, and had to sit down in the bay seat to convince myself I was not already dreaming.

But I was not.

I was very much awake.

There was no sign of Wulfrun. Instead, on the new grave, clearly illuminated by the moon, were a man and a woman in an ardent embrace. He was dark-haired with an aquiline nose, wearing a royal courtier's clothes of centuries ago. She had a gown of iridescent blue embroidered with gleaming gold threads, and the most ravishing tresses of flowing red hair. They held each other closely and tightly, kissing like I have never seen two lovers embrace before.

Along with several of the good sisters at Shaftesbury, I had known love before finding the grace of the cloister. Unlike many of the good brothers at Glastonbury, who had been brought up since childhood in the monastery, our lives as women before taking the veil had been full, with the usual range of marriages, romances, excitements, and disappointments. But I had never seen any love like that which was now before me, burning with the intensity of a lifetime of yearning, and denial.

I gazed on, spellbound for several minutes, aware of the great, brooding tor in the background overlooking the scene. Then a cloud moved over the moon, and the graveyard was cast into darkness. I could no longer see the lovers but, after a few moments, I heard what sounded like the click of the graveyard's gate latch. When, several minutes later, the cloud moved on and the graves were again bathed in moonlight, the couple had gone.

I lay on the bed, my mind filled with the wonder of their embrace. The words of the Song of Songs came to me as I was overtaken by sleep. *Let him kiss me with the kisses of his mouth, for your love is better than wine . . . Your lips, my bride, drip as the honeycomb . . . For love is as strong as death . . . its flames are flames of fire.*

The hour for Vigils had passed but, when the Lauds bell rang just before dawn, I threw on my habit and shoes and ran down to the graveyard rather than the church. I let myself in through the gate, and made quickly for the fresh grave. There, on the newly turned earth, lay the silver chains that had bound Guinevere and Lancelot.

I stared at the discarded fetters, lost for a moment in the memory of the lovers, when I was startled by a sound from behind the headstone, and peered around it to see Wulfrun, pale and barely conscious.

"Where are they?" I asked her urgently.

"Where they are meant to be." She barely breathed the words.

I pressed her for more details, but she had slipped into insentience. Panicking, I ran to Lauds and fetched Brother Anselm, who picked

Wulfrun up and carried her to the public infirmary, where he tended to her for the next ten days until she had recovered the strength to return home. I delayed my journey back to Shaftesbury in order to speak with her, and went to bid her farewell as she set out.

"In the church, you did an extraordinary thing that I do not comprehend," I started. "And then, in the graveyard, you did an equally extraordinary thing that I also do not comprehend."

Wulfrun smiled, and now I could see the strength that I had not been able to perceive in the moonlight. It was a fortitude that seemed to come from deep within and from down the ages, animating her whole being. "Yes, you do, my lady abbess." Her full gaze met mine. "Unlike the abbot and the priest, you, with your many experiences, do understand." And with that, she was gone.

There is not much more for me to tell.

Abbot Henry had the bones of the horses and riders ground up and burnt, then he reconsecrated the abbey church to cleanse it of the defilement and ancient arts it had hosted. The monks procured a skeleton of a large man and a woman, and proudly put them on display as the bones of Arthur and Guinevere, attracting large numbers of tourists whose generosity helped pay for rebuilding the abbey. And there the matter was concluded.

There has not been a time when I have not thought of events in the abbey that day. Did God send Wulfrun to us? Or was she — and the powers she commanded — beyond His law and the teachings of His saints? She said I understood and, at times, I think I do, but at others it is a mystery that wreaths me in doubts. She undoubtedly was motivated by love, and so must have been of God. And yet not in any way the Scriptures understand. After the passage of so much time — and I have had decades to reflect on it — this is what haunts me the most.

Unfortunately for Abbot Henry, he died four years later, and no one was ever able to tell me the cause.

And so, with many years having passed since the events, memories of the ghouls and the lovers always bring me to the same passage of Scripture, which I now see in so many more colours than ever I did before. *Remember now your Creator in the days of your youth, for the dust will return to the earth as it was, and the Spirit will return to God who gave it.*

Amen.

 —————— oOo ——————

As I completed the final page of Mary's *Chronica*, I realized the sun was now setting and I had quite forgotten lunch and the Museum's unparalleled tea room. The building would soon close, and I slumped back into my chair, exhausted, and physically and emotionally drained, quite unable to process the enormities of what I had read. I numbly handed the volume back to the assistant at the Enquires Desk, and asked for it to be held overnight for me to consult again in the morning.

That night I slept fitfully. My mind filled with phantasmagorical images from Mary's terrifying tale, and I awoke early, unrefreshed. Once dressed, I read over my Latin transcription and, to my horror, discovered that the manuscript's loose title page had found its way into the sheaf of foolscap papers onto which I had been copying the text.

My preparations for returning to the Museum were interrupted by the telephone and a message ordering me to report immediately to Bethnal Green ambulance pool. I reluctantly put the Museum papers away, changed into my olive ATS uniform, and caught the underground east.

The Nazi onslaught on London intensified for a period, and over the next three weeks I was unable to find a day to return to the Museum. Eventually, however, I had a day's furlough, and was outside the Museum early. When its doors opened I was first in, and made straight for the Enquiries Desk, my face burning at the prospect of being reported to the police for theft. But no such ordeal awaited me. The assistant on duty simply accepted my chit requesting *Cotton Cleopatra F VIII*, and I took my seat. Volumes were usually delivered within twenty minutes but, after three quarters of an hour, nothing had appeared. When the hour had passed, I returned to the Enquiries Desk to ask if there was any difficulty. The assistant disappeared to investigate, and returned empty handed. He gave me back my chit, and politely informed me there was no volume with the class mark *Cotton Cleopatra F VIII*. I assured him categorically there was, whereupon he turned to the shelf behind him and took down Hammer-schmidt-Hummel's printed catalogue of the Cottonian collection and pointed to the index page, which — to my bewilderment — listed the final volume in the Cleopatra series as F VII.

Stunned, I returned to my seat to retrieve the papers from my bag. I handed the assistant the carbon of my original order chit showing I received *Cotton Cleopatra F VIII* on the 15th of April 1941. I also gave him my transcription of Mary's *Chronica*. And I sheepishly produced the loose title page of vellum, explaining that I had taken it in error and was going to place it back into the manuscript. To my astonishment, he merely shrugged, and said he could not help as the volume did not exist.

I pleaded with the assistant to send someone down into the stacks to double check. Eventually he agreed but, after several hours, returned with the message that a thorough search had been conducted and the answer was the same: the Museum had no knowledge of a *Cotton Cleopatra F VIII*.

I think I grew a little frenzied for several weeks. I returned to the Museum every day I was able to and requested the volume, but the answer was invariably the same. I admit that I became obsessed. I ordered the full run of Cotton Cleopatra f volumes to see if f viii would appear after consulting the others in order. I arrived at the same time as on the first occassion, wore the same clothes, and sat at the same desk. I put in a request exactly a month after first reading it. Then six months. Then a year. To my intense frustration, all these approaches yielded nothing.

I cannot recall when, but I eventually realized that the day I originally consulted the volume was the Tuesday following Easter, which was exactly the same day on which, centuries ago in 1191, the terrible events Mary related had taken place at Glastonbury Abbey. And so I became fixated on that date, returning to the Museum on the 15th of April each year. Yet still the volume did not reappear.

Then, one day, while looking through Clémencet's invaluable 1750 edition of *L'art de vérifier les dates*, I realized how foolish I had been. I had neglected to take into account the annual calendrical movement of Easter. It was then suddenly clear to me that the manuscript would not reappear on the anniversary of the 15th of April, or even the anniversary of the 23rd of April, which was the date of the Tuesday after Easter in 1191. Rather, it would be on whatever changing date the Tuesday after Easter fell in any given year. Still, however, the manuscript did not reappear.

The final piece of the jigsaw only slotted into place several decades later. I was staring at tables I had drawn up of dates, still trying feverishly to find correlations, when suddenly I saw that the year in which I had first read the manuscript, 1941, was the 850th anniversary of the original events of 1191. In some unfathomable way I instantly knew that the two must somehow be connected. So I reasoned the manuscript must, most likely, appear in a fifty-year cycle. The next occasion will therefore be 1991, when the Tuesday after Easter will fall on the 2nd of April. And the one after that will be the 21st of April 2041. I will not still be alive, but I trust someone who has read these papers will have the curiosity to visit the Museum and order the volume which, I am certain, will reappear.

And that is all I can tell you of these affairs.

I am enclosing two additional items for your reference. One is my original Latin transcription. I am sending it to you in the hope you might consider publishing it, perhaps in a parallel English-Latin edition. For scholars at least, the Latin version will be of immense interest. I am also enclosing the original title page of Mary's *Chronica*, which the Museum expressed no interest in retaining, and so it has remained with my papers. You may have it examined, and any expert of your choice will confirm to you what I have been absolutely certain of from its palaeography: that it is an original late twelfth- or early thirteenth-century document. Perhaps it will help convince your editorial board that I am not insane, and that these events really did take place as I have described them.

I remain, yours faithfully,

Iana Jenkins, F.B.A., D.PHIL.

Publisher's Postscript

By the time this undated letter was discovered among the papers of Dr Jenkins, the publishers to which she had addressed it, Watkins & Brown of Cecil Court, London, had ceased to operate.

The letter eventually found its way to us, and we now publish it, not in a scholarly edition with the Latin transcription — we leave that to an academic press — but just as Dr Jenkins wrote it.

In making the decision to publish, our editors undertook intensive research around the details set out in the letter in order to assess its trustworthiness. The following may, therefore, be of interest to readers.

The "Cotton Cleopatra F VIII" Manuscript

1. The British Museum's "Cotton Cleopatra F" manuscripts end at class mark F VII. They are now housed in the British Library. Our attempts to locate F VIII have not been successful.

2. The single leaf of vellum sent by Dr Jenkins to Watkins & Brown has been examined by experts in palaeography and carbon dating. Both place it at the time of Mary of Shaftesbury in the late-twelfth and early-thirteenth centuries. Detailed analysis of the pollen and other biomarkers on it suggest a provenance in the West of England.

Glastonbury Abbey

3. Glastonbury Abbey was badly ravaged by fire in 1184. The Lady Chapel was rebuilt in a spectacular gothic style by 1186. Written sources say that the monks dug up the remains of Arthur and Guinevere in 1191. The tourist revenues from visitors coming to see the bones of Arthur and Guinevere paid for the remainder of the abbey's rebuilding works.

Persons

4. Mary of Shaftesbury was the daughter of Geoffrey of Anjou, also known as Geoffrey Plantagenet. She was half-sister to King Henry II of England, and aunt to Kings Richard the Lionheart and John Lackland. It is not known whether she was born in her father's lands in France, or in England. She was appointed abbess of Shaftesbury perhaps in 1181. She is considered by many to be the contemporary poetess writing in England calling herself "Marie de France". Mary died in 1216.

5. Henry of Sully was a Cluniac monk, appointed abbot of Glastonbury from 1189 to 1193, and then bishop of Worcester. He died in 1195, four years after the exhumation of Arthur and Guinevere.

6. Gerald of Wales — often known by his Latin name, Giraldus Cambrensis — was appointed a royal chaplain to King Henry II in 1185. and continued to serve at King Richard the Lionheart's court until *circa* 1196. He says he was present in 1191 for the exhumation of Arthur and Guinevere at Glastonbury. In two of

his works — the *Liber de principis instructione* (On the Instruction of Princes, written *circa* 1194–8) and the *Speculum ecclesiae* (Mirror of the Church, written *circa* 1219–23) — he tells the story. In particular, he recounts that:

a. An elderly British bard told King Henry II that Arthur was buried deep in the earth at Glastonbury, in a hollowed-out oak tree, between two stone pyramids. Henry told the abbot of Glastonbury of this.

b. In 1191, under Abbot Henry, the monks excavated, and found a hollowed-out oak tree trunk between two stone pyramids, along with a metal plaque in the shape of a cross with an inscription reading, "*Hic jacet sepultus inclitus rex Arthurus cum Wenneueria vxore sua secunda in insula Auallonia*" (Here in the Isle of Avalon lies buried the renowned King Arthur with Winneveria his second wife).

c. Inside the hollowed-out oak were the bones of an inordinately tall man, along with those of a shorter woman, whose remains still had a tress of intricately braided hair, which crumbled to dust when a monk excitedly picked it up.

Medieval Texts

7. The Welsh monk Nennius was historically thought to have written the *Historia brittonum* (The History of the Britons) around 829/830. The book lists the twelve battles of Arthur, and records that at the Battle of Guinnion Castle Arthur carried an image of Saint Mary ever Virgin on "his shoulders" (almost certainly a scribal error for "his shield"). It also contains accounts of the magical pawprint of his dog, Cabal, and the magical grave of his son, Anir. Most interestingly Nennius describes Arthur as "*dux bellorum*" (leader of the battles) rather than *rex* (king).

8. Geoffrey of Monmouth was a Welsh priest and later bishop of St Asaph. He wrote the *Historia regum britannie* (The History of the Kings of Britain) *circa* 1136. In it, he retells stories of the history of Britain, including the

earliest known account of King Leir and his three daughters Gonorilla, Regau, and Cordeilla, whom Shakespeare made famous in *King Lear*. Geoffrey says that that his source for these stories was "a certain very ancient book in the Brittonic language" passed to him by his friend Walter, archdeacon of Oxford, but no such book has ever been discovered. Geoffrey first told his stories of Merlin in the *Prophetiae merlini* (Prophecies of Merlin), but then told them again in the *Historia*, recounting the incidents of the two dragons, Stonehenge, and Igraine of Tintagel. In Geoffrey's account of events, after Merlin helps Uther rape Igraine, Merlin disappears from the tale, and never features in Arthur's life. That friendship was invented by later writers, who made Merlin chief magician to Arthur's court.

Lightning Source UK Ltd.
Milton Keynes UK
UKHW020715020822
406728UK00009B/1003